Plan of
CHARLESTON HARBOR,
And its fortifications.

Compiled by Elliot & Ames
From Government Surveys.
Boston. 1861.

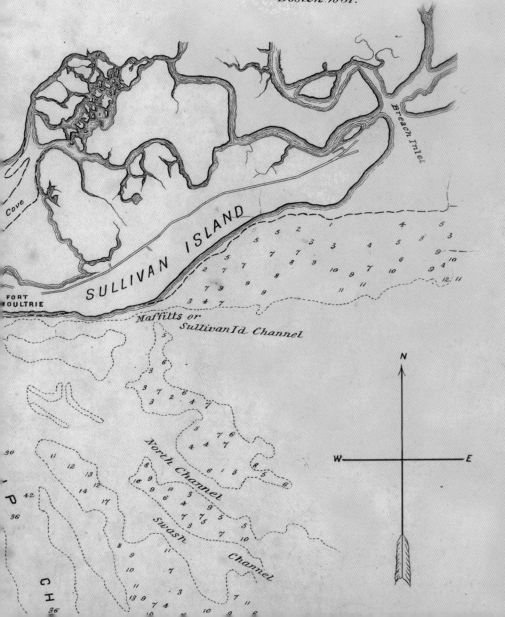

FORT MOULTRIE

SULLIVAN ISLAND

Cove

Breach Inlet

Maffitts or Sullivan Id Channel

North Channel

Swash Channel

N
W — E
S

ROBERT SMALLS.
Captain of the Gunboat "Planter"

Note.

Line of Low Water is represented thus. _ _ _ _

„ Channel „ „ ------------

Small Figures represent depths in feet at Low Water.

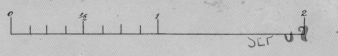

0   ½   1   2

FREEDOM SHIP

DOREEN RAPPAPORT

Illustrated by
CURTIS JAMES

JUMP AT THE SUN

HYPERION BOOKS FOR CHILDREN

NEW YORK

I'm going to tell you a true story, just the way I heard it. It was passed down in my family from my great-great-grandfather. His name was Samuel. I'm named after him.

Great-great-grandfather Samuel and his father were born slaves. During the Civil War, Samuel's father worked on a Confederate steamer out of Charleston, South Carolina. The North and South fought during the Civil War. The Northern states were called the Union. The Southern states were called the Confederacy.

Great-great-grandfather was a little boy during that war, but he remembered it very well. Especially what happened on May 13, 1862!

"*Hold it, move it,*
Hold it, move it . . ."

I swab the deck and listen to Abraham chant as the crew lugs another cannon onto the steamer, the *Planter*. I don't know how they can carry such big heavy things.

"Samuel," Papa calls.

I drop my mop and run as fast as I can to him.

I haven't seen Papa all afternoon. He's been with Robert the whole time. Robert's the real pilot of the ship, even though the captain calls him a wheelman.

"You been workin' real hard, Samuel," Robert says. "Your papa thought you might like to look through these." He holds out his field glasses and we walk out onto the deck. I want to grab the glasses, but I know Papa wouldn't like that, so I reach out real polite-like.

The field glasses are magic. They make faraway look very close. I look up at white, fluffy clouds, then down at seagulls swooping into the blue water. I see many Confederate ships in the harbor. Too many to count. I see the big cannons on Fort Sumter and on Sullivan Island. Beyond the forts, out in the Atlantic Ocean, are Union warships. If only we could get to them, we'd be free.

Suddenly, Papa and Robert stiffen to attention. The captain and his officers are leaving the boat. Robert runs after them and salutes them. When they're out of sight, Abraham comes running.

"Captain sure is mad at us," Abraham says. There's a big grin on Abraham's face. "Says we all lazy and no good. He says those four cannons shoulda been loaded on the ship by now. And if they ain't on by tomorrow mornin', he gonna whip us."

Papa laughs. "If he can catch us," he says.

"What do you mean, Papa?"

"Nothin' son. Only jokin'." Papa is all business now. "Go tell your mama I won't be comin' home tonight. I have to guard the ship."

"Can I stay with ya'll, Papa?"

"Not tonight."

There's no protesting. When Papa says no, it's no.

Someone is tapping me on the shoulder. "Samuel, git up." The lilting voice sounds like Mama's, but I'm too sleepy to want to find out. The hand taps a little harder. I open my eyes. The room is pitch black. It's got to be the middle of the night.

"Samuel, put on ya clothes real silent-like," Mama says.

"Why?" I ask, in between yawns.

"No questions now. Just do as I say."

I slip into my clothes. Mama folds my white bedsheet in half, then in half again. Again and again, until it's a small square. She slips it into a sack and opens the front door. The dark sky has only a sprinkling of stars. Mama looks both ways. I tug at her skirt. "Where we goin'?"

"Hush, no more talkin'. You'll find out soon enough."

Mama races ahead. It's hard keeping up with her. She seems to be flying, not walking.

Footsteps. Coming fast behind us. Someone is trying to catch up to us. Please don't let it be the police. I'm sure Mama doesn't have a pass for us to be out. If the police find us out with no pass, they'll throw us in jail. And tell Master Smith, who'll surely whip us.

The footsteps are on top of us now.

"Lavinia," someone whispers.

Who is this person who knows Mama's name?

Mama and I spin around to see who owns the whisper.

It's Robert Smalls's wife, Hannah, and her two children.

What are they doing out here in the middle of the night? What are we doing out here?

Without saying a word, Mama takes Hannah's baby in her arms. She walks even faster now down the street, toward Cooper River. A lantern is glowing on the deck of a small boat. Mama starts running. Mrs. Smalls runs after her. To the dock. Across a small plank. Onto a small merchant ship.

"Downstairs," the man whispers.
"The others are already here."

In the dark cabin below I count four
other women. One is Abraham's wife.
I don't know the other women but Mama
must because she hugs each one. Then
she wraps her arms around me and whispers,
"Soon we gonna be free."

Free? I want to ask Mama how, but
something tells me she'd hush me.

I feel the boat moving. It's leaving
the dock. I want to ask Mama where it's
going, but something tells me she'd hush
me about this, too.

The boat moves slowly through the water. It is no more than a few minutes later when the man from the deck sticks his head into the cabin. "They're here," he says.

Who are they? Again, no time for questions. Hurry, hurry. Up the stairs. To the deck. I see a rowboat coming toward us. Closer. Closer. It's Papa! Papa and Abraham!

"Gently, gently," Papa whispers, as I step into the boat. Mama follows. Then, one by one, everyone else. The boat rocks back and forth with each new person.

Papa dips the oars into the water. He pulls them hard, but there is no splashing, only the tiniest of ripples.

Pull, pull. Faster, faster. We're heading out of the harbor. We glide along. Soon we are alongside the *Planter*. One by one, we jump onto the deck.

Papa runs to the pilothouse. I race after him. Abraham hoists the Confederate flag on one pole and the state flag, the Palmetto, on another.

Robert turns the wheel, and the *Planter* creeps down the river. We pass other Confederate ships anchored in the harbor. Robert turns the wheel again. He's steering us past Fort Sumter and its big cannons. Won't the guard wonder why we're moving and all the other ships in the harbor are still?

"Lord, please stand over us and guide us to freedom as you did the Israelites," Robert says.

Tooooot! Tooooot! Toot! He pulls the whistle cord, asking for permission to leave the harbor. I hold my breath.

Tooooot! Tooooot! Toot!

We have permission! The *Planter* plows through the water toward Sullivan Island and its big cannons. My knees are shaking. But Robert doesn't look at all afraid as he pulls the whistle cord a second time.

Almost instantly they toot back permission.

"One more fort to go," Papa says.

"Remember, Gabriel," Robert says to Papa. "If we don't make it past Fort Moultrie, we blow up the ship."

"Agreed."

"Blow up the ship?" I scream.

"Quiet, boy," Papa says.

Robert tells Papa to take the wheel. He puts on the captain's jacket, and his straw hat. He folds his arms across his chest and walks back and forth. He's not walking like he usually walks. He's walking like . . . like the captain. He's pretending to be the captain. Can he really fool the soldiers?

Tooooot! Tooooot! Toot! Papa signals for permission.

I squeeze my eyelids as tight as I can.

The sentry sounds the all clear. The *Planter* picks up speed and we surge past the fort. Straight out toward the Atlantic Ocean. Straight toward the Union warships.

Suddenly lights flash from Fort Moultrie toward Fort Sumter, then from Sumter back to Charleston. They've realized that we're heading toward the Union warships.

"Papa, Papa, they're gonna shoot us!"

"We're too far away for that to happen, son," he says confidently. "But the Union ships will fire on us unless—"

Papa races to the flagpole. He pulls hard on the ropes holding up the Confederate flag. Down it comes. Abraham takes down the Palmetto. Suddenly Mama is at Papa's side. She gives him my white bedsheet. He ties it to the flagpole.

"What are you doing?" I ask.

"A white sheet means surrender. When the Union officers see it, they won't fire at us."

Up, up, we pull the bedsheet. I wait for it to billow but it just droops.

Suddenly the *Planter* swings around as Robert steers it into the wind, and the bedsheet flares out. Now we're moving full speed ahead, straight toward the Union ships. There are one, two, three, four . . . ten Union ships.

What's that noise? Drums! The Union sailors are beating drums. They're getting ready to shoot at us. *Oh, no! Don't they see my white bedsheet?*

One of the Union ships moves out ahead of the others toward us. Closer. Closer. I see its guns sticking out through the portholes.

I open my mouth to shout, "No, don't shoot," but no words come out.

Robert yells, "The *Planter*, out of Charleston, come to join the Union fleet! And we've brought you Confederate cannons and a lot of ammunition."

"Hold your fire!" a Union officer shouts.

Mama runs to Papa and me. They press me to them. Tears stream down their faces.

"We're free now, Samuel, we're free!" Papa says.

Free! Free! The word covers my tongue with happiness.

AUTHOR'S NOTE

This book is based on a true incident in American history. I reconstructed the event from newspaper accounts of the period and from details given in *From Slavery to Service: Robert Smalls, 1839–1915,* written by Okon Edet Uya, published by Oxford University Press, 1971. The family in my book is fictional.

On May 13, 1862, twenty-three-year-old Robert Smalls and the nine-member slave crew of the *Planter* kidnapped the ship and delivered it, its cannons, and ammunition to the Union Army. Robert Smalls was the ship's pilot. John Smalls (no relation) and Alfred Gradine were ship engineers. Abraham Jackson, Gabriel Turno, William Morrison, Samuel Chisolm, Abraham Allston, and David Jones were crew members. Five black women and three children also escaped. Two of the children were Robert and Hannah Smalls'. I was unable to find out who the other child was, so I took the liberty of naming him Samuel.

News of this daring achievement spread through the North and South. The loss of the *Planter* devastated the Confederacy, for it was needed to carry supplies and troops along the Carolina coast. Northerners applauded the crew's courage and ingenuity. Smalls was declared a hero, appointed as a pilot in the U.S. Navy, and assigned to the *Planter.*

Robert Smalls went with Reverend Mansfield French to Washington, D.C., to persuade President Lincoln to allow African Americans to join the Union Army. During a meeting with Secretary of War Edwin M. Stanton, Reverend French argued that there were other courageous black men like Smalls. After Lincoln finally allowed blacks to join the army, Smalls spoke at churches and schools to encourage other runaway slaves to join the fight for freedom.

Smalls participated in seventeen naval battles during the Civil War. On December 1, 1863, the *Planter* was sailing through Stono River, near Folly Creek in South Carolina. Under heavy Confederate fire, the white commanding officer panicked and wanted to surrender. Smalls took control of the ship, returned fire, and brought it out of firing range and back to port. He was promoted to captain of the *Planter.*

After the war ended, Smalls was elected as a delegate to the state's constitutional convention, which rewrote South Carolina's constitution to allow blacks equal education for their children, equal protection under the law, the right to vote, and the right to run for public office. He was elected to the state legislature. Two years later, he was elected to the state senate. He served five terms in the U.S. House of Representatives. In 1887, he became the customs collector for Beaufort for the next twenty-four years.

TO FIND OUT MORE ABOUT ROBERT SMALLS AND OTHER BRAVE AFRICAN AMERICANS READ:

Abraham, Philip. *Harriet Tubman*. New York: Scholastic Library Publishing, 2002.

Cooper, Michael L. *From Slave to Civil War Hero: The Life and Times of Robert Smalls*. New York: Dutton/Lodestar Books, 1994.

Edwards, Pamela Duncan. *Barefoot: Escape on the Underground Railroad*. Illustrated by Henry Cole. New York: HarperCollins, 1998.

Hopkinson, Deborah. *Under the Quilt of Night*. Illustrated by James E. Ransome. New York: Simon & Schuster, 2001.

Kulling, Monica. *Escape North! The Story of Harriet Tubman*. Illustrated by Teresa Flavin. New York: Random House, 2000.

Levine, Ellen. *If You Traveled on the Underground Railroad*. Illustrated by Elroy Freem. New York: Scholastic, 1998.

Miller, Edward A. *Gullah Statesman: Robert Smalls from Slavery to Congress, 1839-1915*. Columbia, SC: University of South Carolina Press, 1995.

Rappaport, Doreen. *Freedom River*. Illustrated by Bryan Collier. New York: Jump at the Sun, 2000.
———. *No More! Stories and Songs of Slave Resistance*. Illustrated by Shane W. Evans. Cambridge, MA: Candlewick Press, 2002.

Simon, Barbara Brooks. *Escape to Freedom: The Underground Railroad Adventures of Callie and William*. Washington, DC: National Geographic Society, 2003.

Uya, Okon Edet. *From Slavery to Public Service: Robert Smalls, 1839-1915*. New York: Oxford University Press, 1971.

WEB SITES

www.robertsmalls.org/
www.beaufort-sc.com/history/smalls.htm
www.history.navy.mil/photos/pers-us/uspers-s/r-smalls.htm
www.constitutioncenter.org/timeline/html/cw05_12032.html
www.africawithin.com/bios/robert_smalls.htm
www.schistory.org

*For Tyler Rosegarten
with love and hugs* —D.R.

*In memory of my father,
Willie James* —C.J.

For information address Hyperion Books for Children,
114 Fifth Avenue, New York, New York 10011-5690.

Endpaper map of Charleston Harbor and picture
of Robert Smalls from the Collections
of the South Carolina Historical Society.

Printed in Singapore
First Edition
1 2 3 4 5 6 7 8 9 10
This book is set in 14 pt. Letterpress Bold.
ISBN 0-7868-0645-1
Reinforced binding
Library of Congresss Cataloging-in-Publication Data on file.
Visit www.hyperionbooksforchildren.com

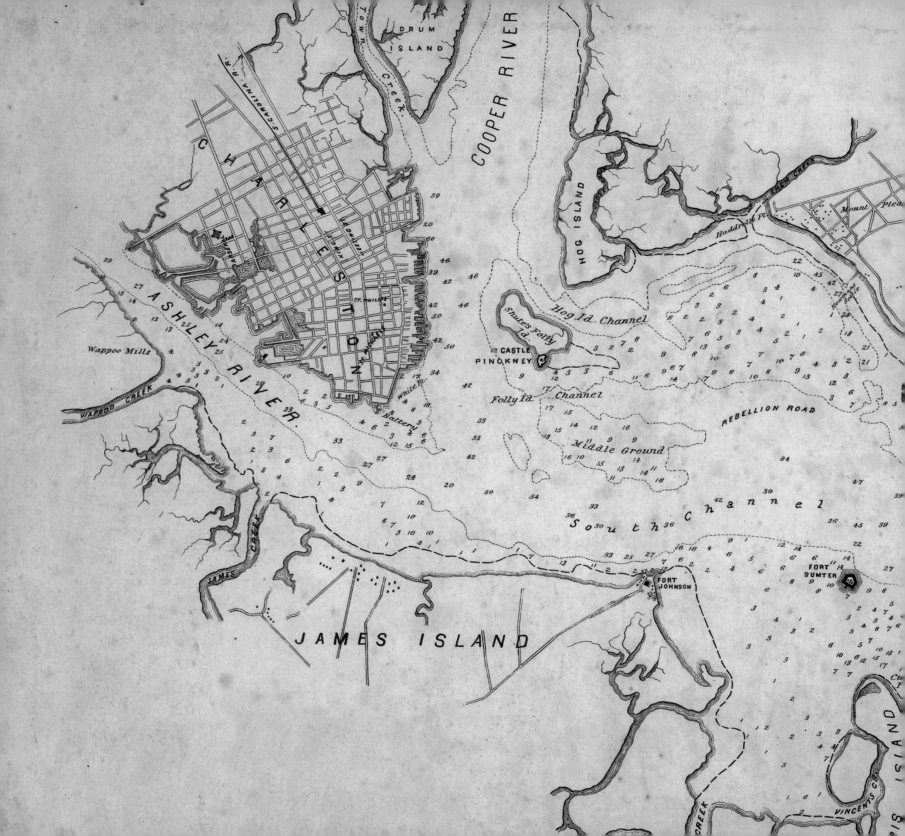